Let's Catch a Rainbow!

Written by Mary Roulston
Illustrated by Juanbjuan Oliver

Collins

What's in this story?

Listen and say

rainbow
jump
run

Fatma says, “Look there!”

Matt says, “It’s a picture.”
Anna says, “No, it’s a rainbow!”

Matt says, “It’s got lots of colours. Red, orange, yellow, green, blue and purple!”

Matt says, “I want to catch the rainbow.”

Anna says, “OK. Run!”

They are running very fast, but they can't catch the rainbow.

Matt says, “Stop! I’m hot.”

Matt says, “I want the rainbow!”

Fatma says, “I know. Let’s jump.”

Matt says, “Yes! We can jump and catch the rainbow!”

The children are jumping.

Anna helps Matt, but Matt can't catch the rainbow.

Matt says, “Why can’t we catch the rainbow?”

Fatma says, “I’m sorry, Matt.”

Anna says, “Let’s go home.”

Bye-bye, rainbow!

Anna says, “Here’s some water.”
Fatma says, “Thank you.”

Matt puts his drink in the sun.

Fatma says, "Look at the wall.
There's a rainbow!"

Matt says, “Yes! Red, orange, yellow, green, blue and purple.”

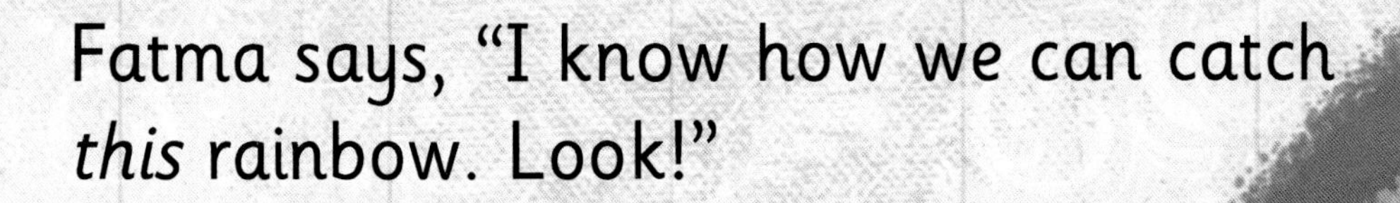
Fatma says, "I know how we can catch *this* rainbow. Look!"

Fatma says, “Do this, Matt.”

Matt says, “Wow! I’ve got a rainbow!”

Picture dictionary

Listen and repeat 

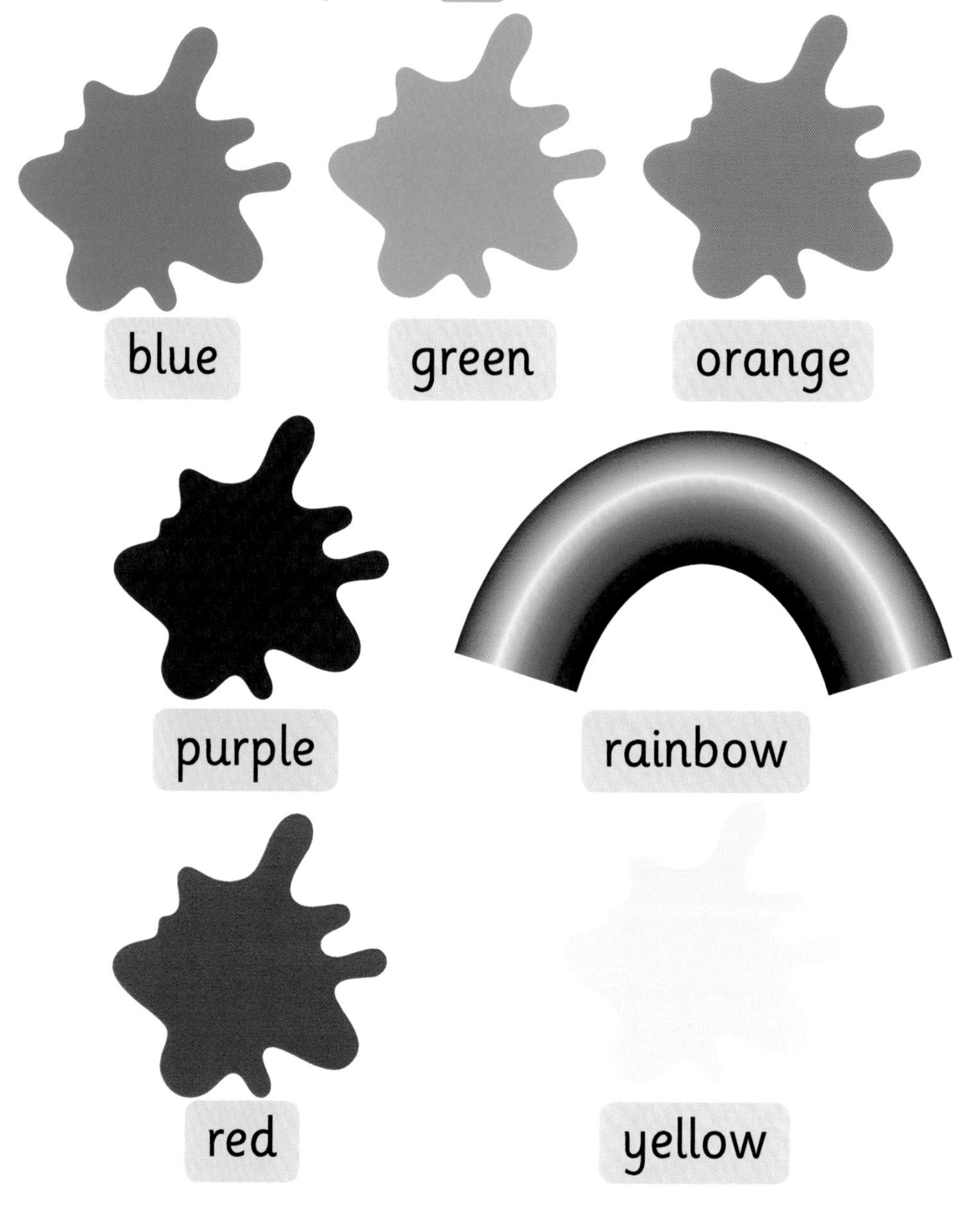

1 Look and order the story

2 Listen and say  

Download a reading guide for parents and teachers at www.collins.co.uk/839700

Collins

Published by Collins
An imprint of HarperCollins*Publishers*
Westerhill Road
Bishopbriggs
Glasgow
G64 2QT

HarperCollins *Publishers*
Macken House,
39/40 Mayor Street Upper,
Dublin 1
D01 C9W8
Ireland

William Collins' dream of knowledge for all began with the publication of his first book in 1819.

A self-educated mill worker, he not only enriched millions of lives, but also founded a flourishing publishing house. Today, staying true to this spirit, Collins books are packed with inspiration, innovation and practical expertise. They place you at the centre of a world of possibility and give you exactly what you need to explore it.

10 9 8 7 6 5 4 3 2 1

ISBN 978-0-00-839700-5

www.collins.co.uk/elt

British Library Cataloguing in Publication Data

A catalogue record for this publication is available from the British Library.

Author: Mary Roulston
Illustrator: Juanbjuan Oliver (Beehive)
Series editor: Rebecca Adlard
Publishing manager: Lisa Todd
Product managers: Jennifer Hall and Caroline Green
In-house editor: Alma Puts Keren
Project manager: Emily Hooton
Editor: Tessie Papadopoulou-Dalton
Proofreaders: Natalie Murray and Michael Lamb
Cover designer: Kevin Robbins
Typesetter: 2Hoots Publishing Services Ltd
Audio produced by id audio, London
Reading guide author: Emma Wilkinson
Production controller: Rachel Weaver
Printed and bound by: Pureprint, UK

This book contains FSC™ certified paper and other controlled sources to ensure responsible forest management.

For more information visit: www.harpercollins.co.uk/green

Download the audio for this book and a reading guide for parents and teachers at www.collins.co.uk/839700